JENNY'S BIRTHDAY BOOK

by Esther Averill

Harper & Row, Publishers

Copyright, 1954, by Esther Averill
Printed in the United States of America
All rights in this book are reserved

Library of Congress catalog card number: 54-6589

This is the day - the day of days - the birthday of the little shy black cat named Jenny Linsky. Somehow it seems as if the sun were shining and the roses blooming just for her. Outside Jenny's window stand her brothers, Checkers and Edward, ready to take her to a birthday picnic in the park.

The park lies in a busy part

of New York City.

As Jenny and her brothers scamper

through the streets, they watch

carefully for the traffic light — the

green light that means Go!

They pass the flower shop.

Then, at the fish shop, Jenny

meets the twins, Romulus

and Remus, carrying a

birthday present.

"Don't open it until we reach

the park," they say.

The next stop is

the fire house

where...

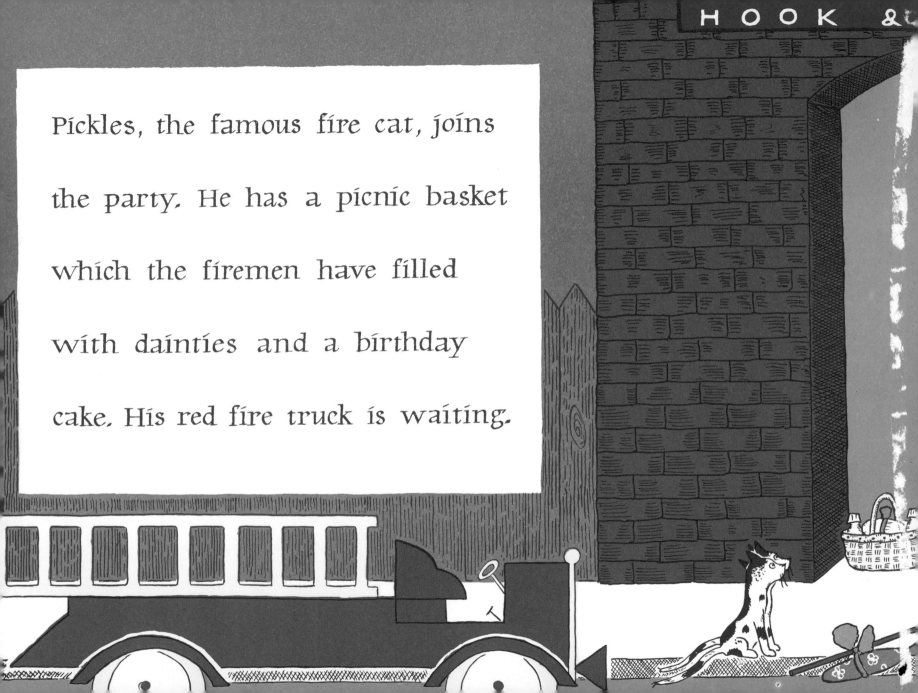

Pickles, the famous fire cat, joins the party. He has a picnic basket which the firemen have filled with dainties and a birthday cake. His red fire truck is waiting.

HOOK &

Pickles starts the engine of his fire truck.

"All aboard for Jenny's birthday picnic in the park!" he cries.

"We mustn't forget Florio," Jenny reminds him as she climbs onto the truck.

While the truck speeds up the avenue towards Florio's house, Pickles sounds his siren.

They pick up Jenny's old
friend, Florio, who wears
an Indian feather in honor
of the birthday.
Then the truck heads for
the flowery park.

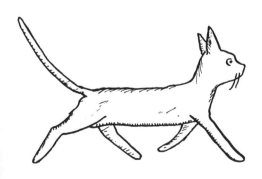

Other cats have heard the siren of the fire truck. These cats, too, are loyal friends of Jenny Linsky. So they follow the trail of the truck and reach the park just as the picnic supper is being spread out on the cool, green grass.

Friends, young and old, troop into the park, singing:

Greetings we bring

And merrily sing

Happy birthday to you!

May dear little Jenny

Have many and many

More birthdays come true.

There is food for all the cats who come a-running.

The twins have given Jenny a delicious bluefish.

The big moon rises while

the feast is being eaten.

After the feast, Jenny's friends gather around her.

"Jenny," they say, "a birthday cat may do whatever she likes best. Please name your wish."

"I'd love to dance," she answers shyly.

"Please name the dance," they beg.

And Jenny cries excitedly, "The sailor's hornpipe!"

They dance the sailor's hornpipe in the moonlit park.

The two big fighters, Sinbad and
The Duke, dance gently with a
little stranger who has wandered
into Jenny's party.

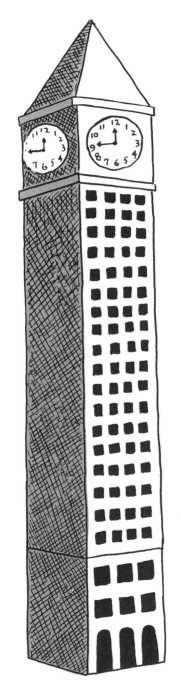

When it grows late, it's time for bed.

The friends pile into Pickles' fire truck,

and he drives the little black cat

to her home.

She thanks them one and all for giving

her a happy birthday. Then...

Jenny waves

good night.

Sleepily she

climbs the

stairs to go

to bed.

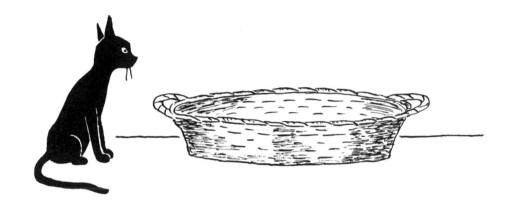

Before she lies down in her basket, Jenny makes a

little prayer: "Please may all cats everywhere have

happy birthdays when their birthdays come."

Soon she is sleeping—

dreaming of her

birthday picnic.

The End

Story books about Jenny and her friends are: *The Cat Club,
The School for Cats, Jenny's First Party, Jenny's Moonlight Adventure,
When Jenny Lost Her Scarf, Jenny's Adopted Brothers,* and *How
the Brothers Joined the Cat Club.*